This book is given with love

_____

_____

To see more of our books, visit us at:
www.PuppyDogsAndIceCream.com

A Mother's Love

The Story of the Midnight Angel

Written by:

Marilee Joy Mayfield

Illustrated by:

Tracy La Rue Hohn

As day turns into evening

And the pale moon finds its place,

You might feel the slightest flutter

Like soft petals on your face.

And when you hear leaves rustling,

A mouse runs a well-worn trail

Though you'll never see his eyes,

His whiskers, or his tail.

Deep in a hidden forest

Seedlings grow without a sound.

But your eyes won't see their presence

Till their stems pop through the ground.

Why is it that when night falls

All the tiny squeaks seem loud?

Nighttime has a secret magic

That gives power to every sound.

So if you hear a crack or creak

When you're snuggled in your bed,

It's NOT a scary monster

It's an angel's wings instead.

Mothers move around the house at night,

Not meaning to make noise.

Sometimes they like to kick up dust

Like playful girls and boys!

For at the stroke of midnight

When you're fast asleep indoors,

She dances through the entrance

Almost gliding on the floors.

She pauses in the kitchen

Puts a stray dish in the sink

And she plays with spoons and teacups

To hear their tinkling clinks.

Candles left upon the mantel

Are a hazard late at night,

So she takes the candle snuffer

And puts out all the lights.

She hears the baby crying

Plants a kiss upon his nose

And rocks him gently in her arms

Till his droopy eyelids close.

In the hallway extra toys are piled

She slides smoothly past them all

Till her arm brushes a bit too close

And the toys roll down and fall.

Each toy gets special treatment

As she puts them all away,

After all they need to sleep well

For tomorrow's time to play.

She checks on Dad who's snoring

Brushes back a lock of hair

Closes up his blinking laptop

As he dreams without a care.

Then, at last, she comes to your room

All is quiet, still, and right

It's all cozy warmth and softness

In the middle of the night.

You know she kissed your forehead
Even though you're sleeping sound,
She prays you dream of angels
Who protect, love, and surround.

So when you're fast asleep at night
She's watching over you,
She guides, protects, and loves you
No matter what you do.

In your dreams you'll feel a message

There are secrets to be found,

For love cannot be seen or heard

And yet it's all around.

Your mom is like an angel

Though you might not see her wings,

And when your life is joyful

It's her happy heart that sings.

A Mother's Love Activity Sheets

We hope you liked reading the story of A Mother's Love.
For some more fun, enjoy the bonus drawing and
worksheets we've included for you!
Don't forget to write your name and age below to help
remember when you did these.

Name: _____

Age: _____ **Date:** _____

Draw Your Family

What Makes Mom Special

Your mom is a very special person, fill in the blanks below
for what makes your mom the best!

♥ My mom's name is _____ .

♥ I like it when she _____ .

♥ My mom is very _____ .

♥ My mom always says _____
_____ .

♥ My mom makes the best _____ .

♥ My mom is really good at _____ .

♥ My favorite thing to do with my mom is _____
_____ .

What Does Mom Do?

Your mom does a lot during the day! Write down what your mom does for your family and what you can do to help.

What Mom does for me:

_____

_____

_____

_____

_____

_____

_____

How I can help Mom:

_____

_____

_____

_____

_____

_____

_____

🐾 Claim Your FREE Gift!

Visit ➤ <u>PDICBooks.com/mother</u>

Thank you for purchasing A Mother's Love,
and welcome to the Puppy Dogs & Ice Cream family.

We're certain you're going to love the little gift we've
prepared for you at the website above.